8/19

Y0-BDF-122

WITHDRAWN

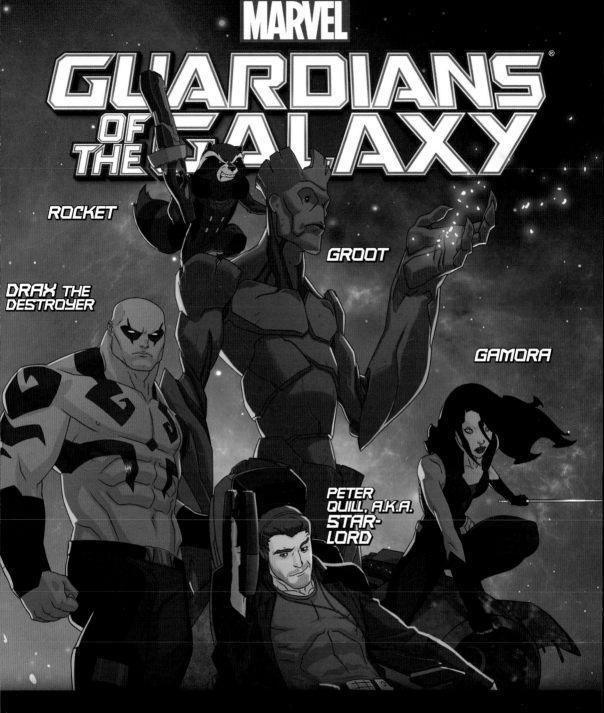

MARVEL
GUARDIANS OF THE GALAXY

ROCKET

GROOT

DRAX THE DESTROYER

GAMORA

PETER QUILL, A.K.A. STAR-LORD

PREVIOUSLY:

The Guardians came into possession of a mysterious
Spartaxan cube that holds a map to an object of immense
power called the Cosmic Seed. Half Spartaxan, Star-Lord is
the only one able to access the map. Now the Guardians must
find the Seed before Thanos does.

Volume 10: Bad Moon Rising
BASED ON THE DISNEY XD ANIMATED TV SERIES

Written by MATT WAYNE   Directed by JEFF WAMESTER
Animation Art Produced by MARVEL ANIMATION STUDIOS   Adapted by JOE CARAMAGNA

Special Thanks to   MARK BASSO & CHRISTINA HARRINGTON editors   MARK PANICCIA senior editor
HANNAH MACDONALD   AXEL ALONSO editor in chief   JOE QUESADA chief creative officer
& PRODUCT FACTORY   DAN BUCKLEY publisher   ALAN FINE executive producer

ABDOBOOKS.COM

Reinforced library bound edition published in 2020 by Spotlight,
a division of ABDO, PO Box 398166, Minneapolis, Minnesota 55439.
Spotlight produces high-quality reinforced library bound editions for
schools and libraries. Published by agreement with Marvel Characters, Inc.

Printed in the United States of America, North Mankato, Minnesota.
042019
092019

THIS BOOK CONTAINS
RECYCLED MATERIALS

© 2020 MARVEL

Library of Congress Control Number: 2018965976

Publisher's Cataloging-in-Publication Data

Names: Caramagna, Joe; Wayne, Matt, authors. | Marvel Animation Studios,
    illustrator.
Title: Bad moon rising / by Joe Caramagna ; Matt Wayne; illustrated by Marvel
    Animation Studios.
Description: Minneapolis, Minnesota : Spotlight, 2020. | Series: Guardians of the
    Galaxy set 3 ; volume 10
Summary: Star-Lord must help the Guardians return to their normal selves after a
    living moon makes them start acting like when they'd first met, and Nebula
    uses the moon's powers to resurrect an old foe.
Identifiers: ISBN 9781532143618 (lib. bdg.)
Subjects: LCSH: Guardians of the Galaxy (Fictitious characters)--Juvenile fiction. |
    Superheroes--Juvenile fiction. | Amnesia--Juvenile fiction. | Graphic novels--
    Juvenile fiction. | Mental healing--Juvenile fiction. | Star-Lord (Fictitious
    character)--Juvenile fiction. | Villains--Juvenile fiction. | Comic books, strips,
    etc--Juvenile fiction.
Classification: DDC 741.5--dc23

Spotlight

A Division of ABDO
abdobooks.com

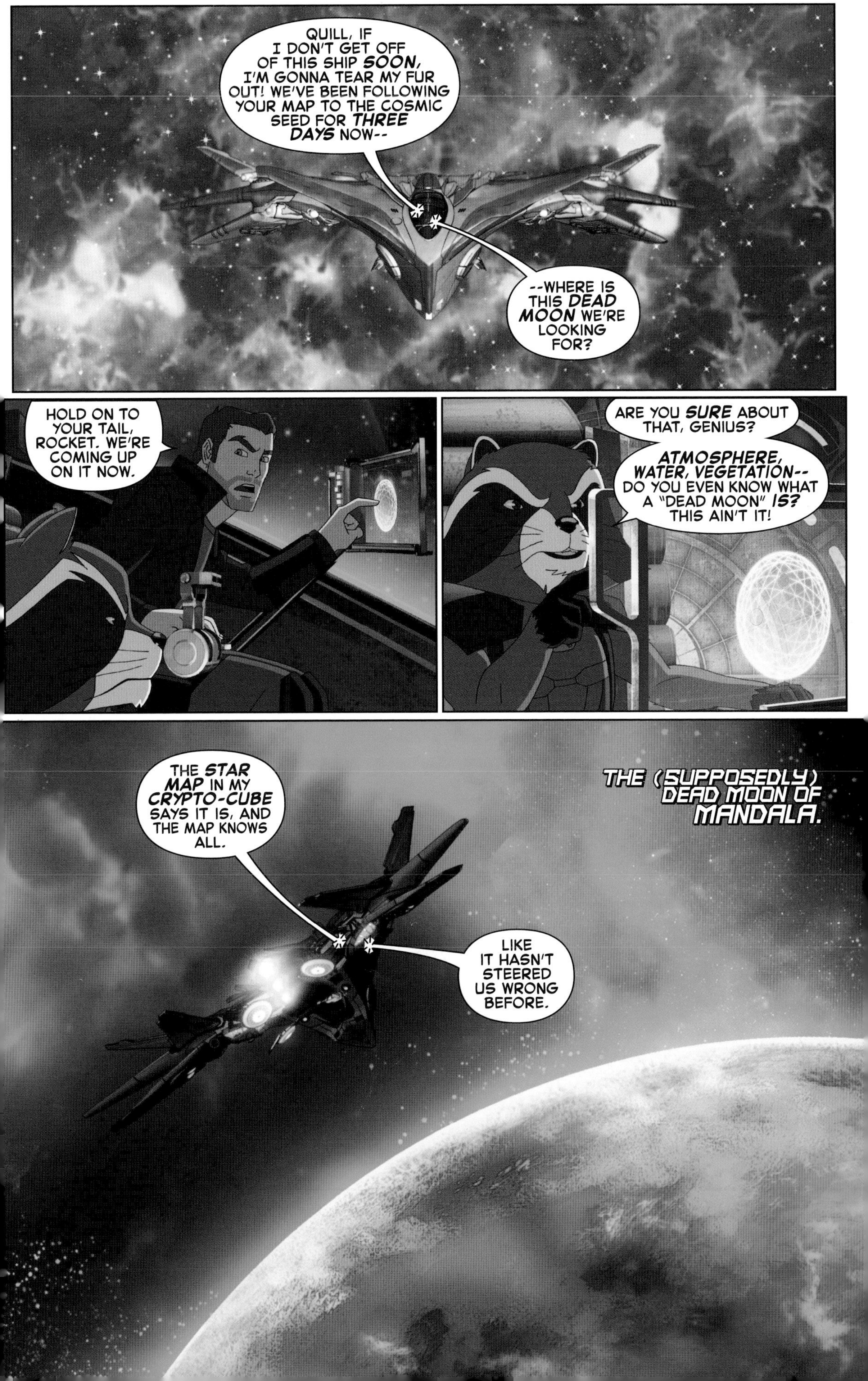
QUILL, IF I DON'T GET OFF OF THIS SHIP SOON, I'M GONNA TEAR MY FUR OUT! WE'VE BEEN FOLLOWING YOUR MAP TO THE COSMIC SEED FOR THREE DAYS NOW--
--WHERE IS THIS DEAD MOON WE'RE LOOKING FOR?
HOLD ON TO YOUR TAIL, ROCKET. WE'RE COMING UP ON IT NOW.
ARE YOU SURE ABOUT THAT, GENIUS?
ATMOSPHERE, WATER, VEGETATION-- DO YOU EVEN KNOW WHAT A "DEAD MOON" IS? THIS AIN'T IT!
THE (SUPPOSEDLY) DEAD MOON OF MANDALA.
THE STAR MAP IN MY CRYPTO-CUBE SAYS IT IS, AND THE MAP KNOWS ALL.
LIKE IT HASN'T STEERED US WRONG BEFORE.

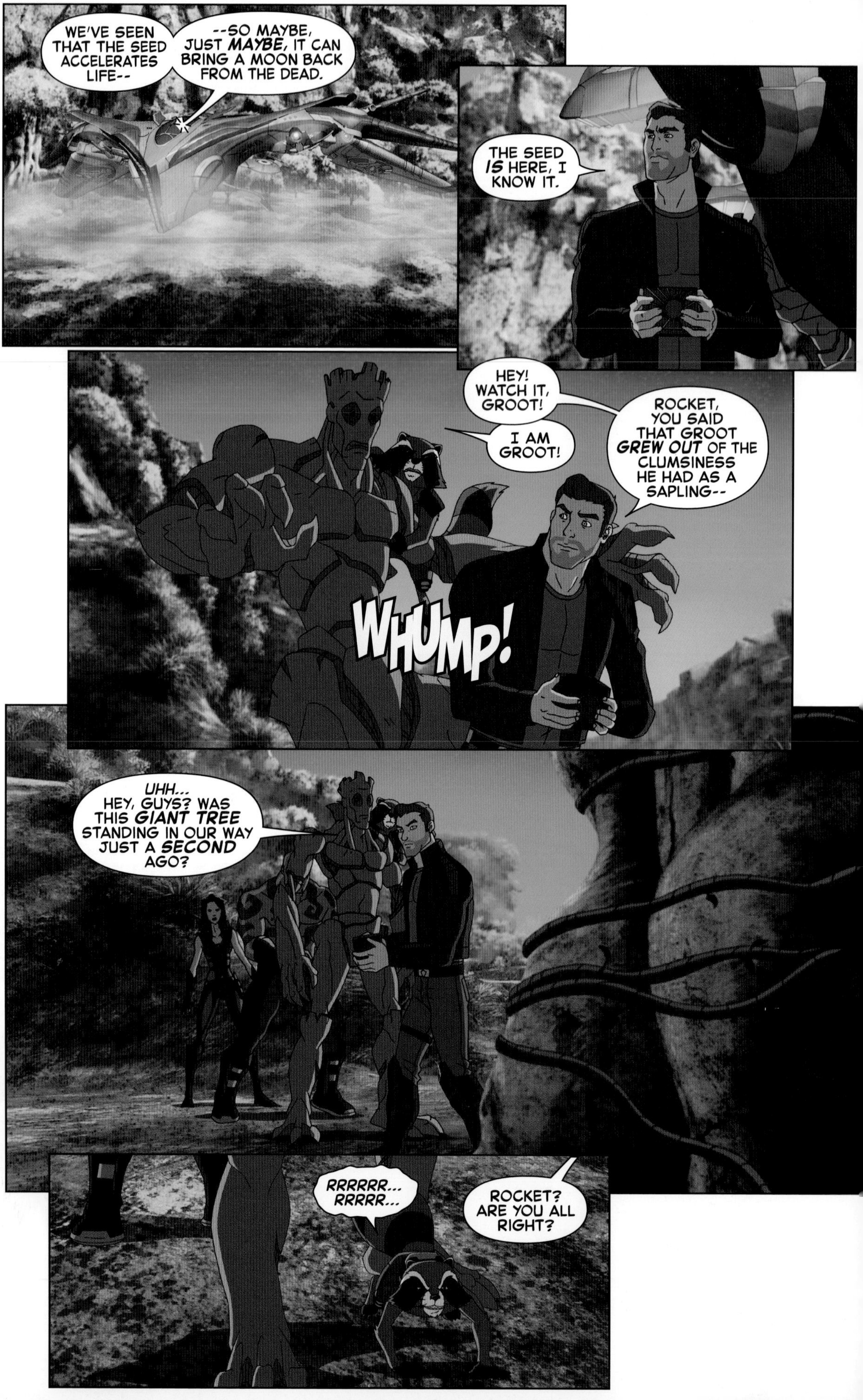
WE'VE SEEN THAT THE SEED ACCELERATES LIFE--
--SO MAYBE, JUST *MAYBE*, IT CAN BRING A MOON BACK FROM THE DEAD.
THE SEED *IS* HERE, I KNOW IT.
HEY! WATCH IT, GROOT!
I AM GROOT!
ROCKET, YOU SAID THAT GROOT *GREW OUT* OF THE CLUMSINESS HE HAD AS A SAPLING--
WHUMP!
UHH... HEY, GUYS? WAS THIS *GIANT TREE* STANDING IN OUR WAY JUST A *SECOND* AGO?
RRRRRR... RRRRR...
ROCKET? ARE YOU ALL RIGHT?

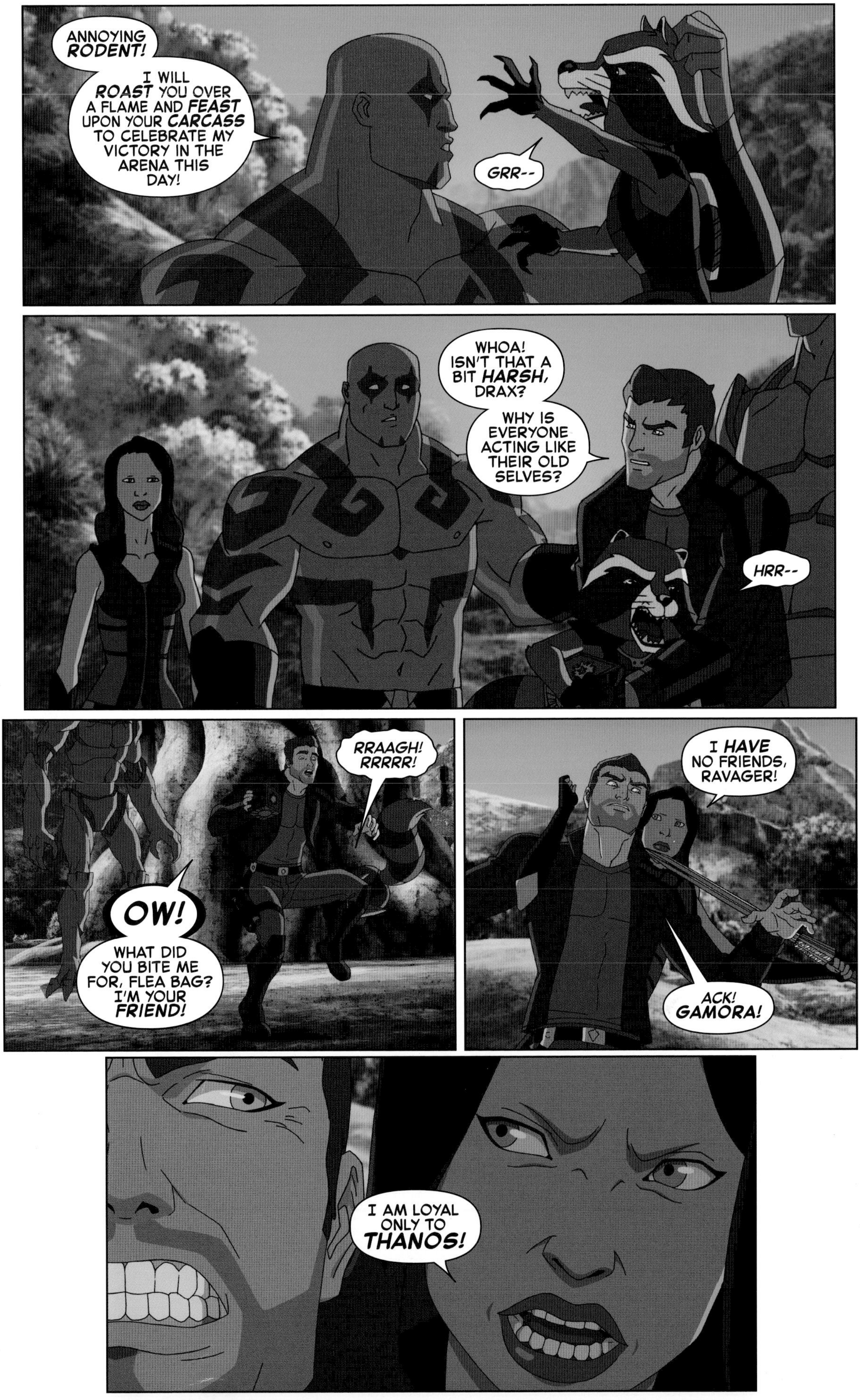

ANNOYING RODENT!
I WILL ROAST YOU OVER A FLAME AND FEAST UPON YOUR CARCASS TO CELEBRATE MY VICTORY IN THE ARENA THIS DAY!
GRR--
WHOA! ISN'T THAT A BIT HARSH, DRAX?
WHY IS EVERYONE ACTING LIKE THEIR OLD SELVES?
HRR--
RRAAGH! RRRRR!
OW!
WHAT DID YOU BITE ME FOR, FLEA BAG? I'M YOUR FRIEND!
I HAVE NO FRIENDS, RAVAGER!
ACK! GAMORA!
I AM LOYAL ONLY TO THANOS!

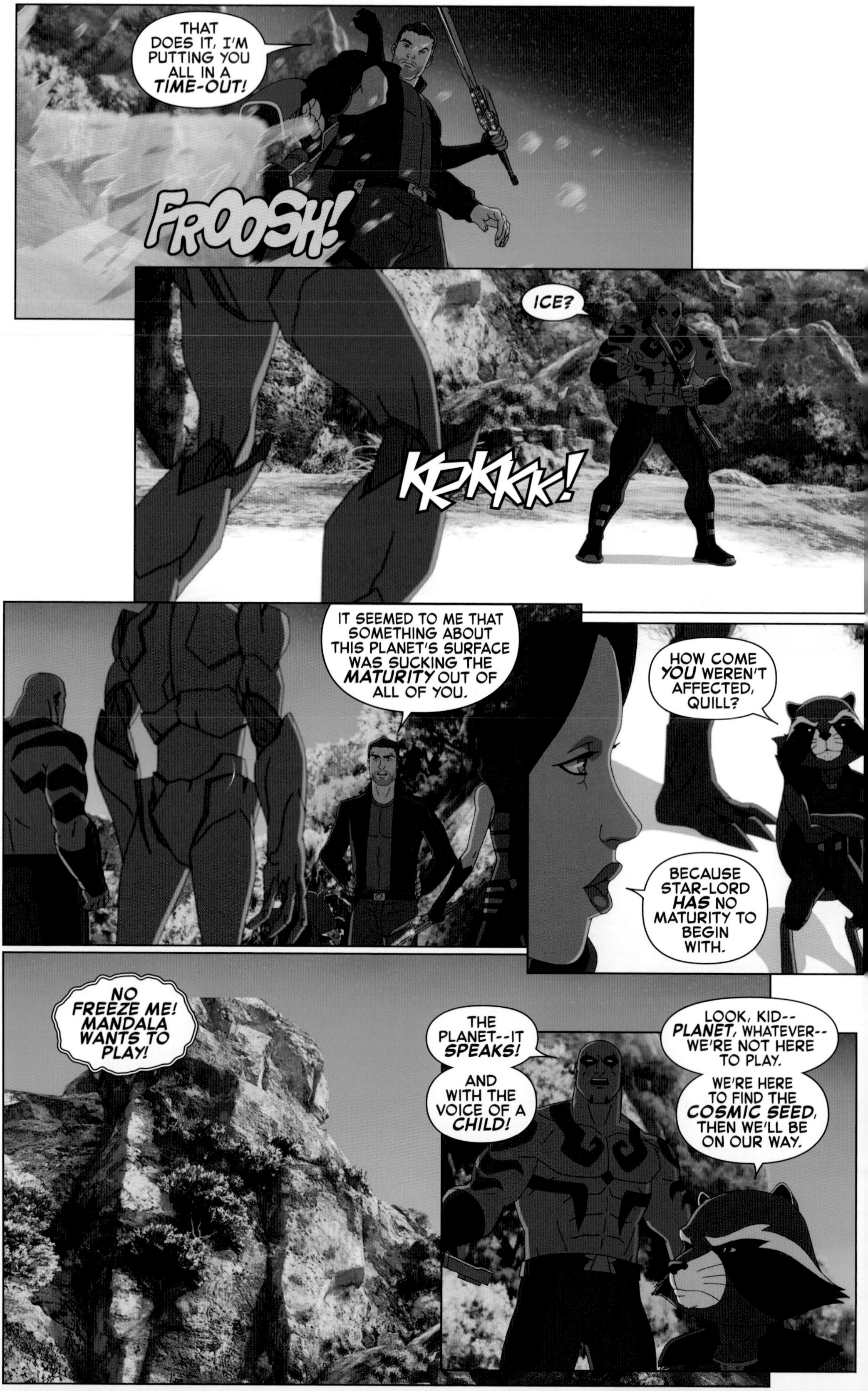
THAT DOES IT, I'M PUTTING YOU ALL IN A TIME-OUT!
FROOSH!
ICE?
KRKKKK!
IT SEEMED TO ME THAT SOMETHING ABOUT THIS PLANET'S SURFACE WAS SUCKING THE MATURITY OUT OF ALL OF YOU.
HOW COME YOU WEREN'T AFFECTED, QUILL?
BECAUSE STAR-LORD HAS NO MATURITY TO BEGIN WITH.
NO FREEZE ME! MANDALA WANTS TO PLAY!
THE PLANET--IT SPEAKS!
AND WITH THE VOICE OF A CHILD!
LOOK, KID--PLANET, WHATEVER--WE'RE NOT HERE TO PLAY.
WE'RE HERE TO FIND THE COSMIC SEED, THEN WE'LL BE ON OUR WAY.

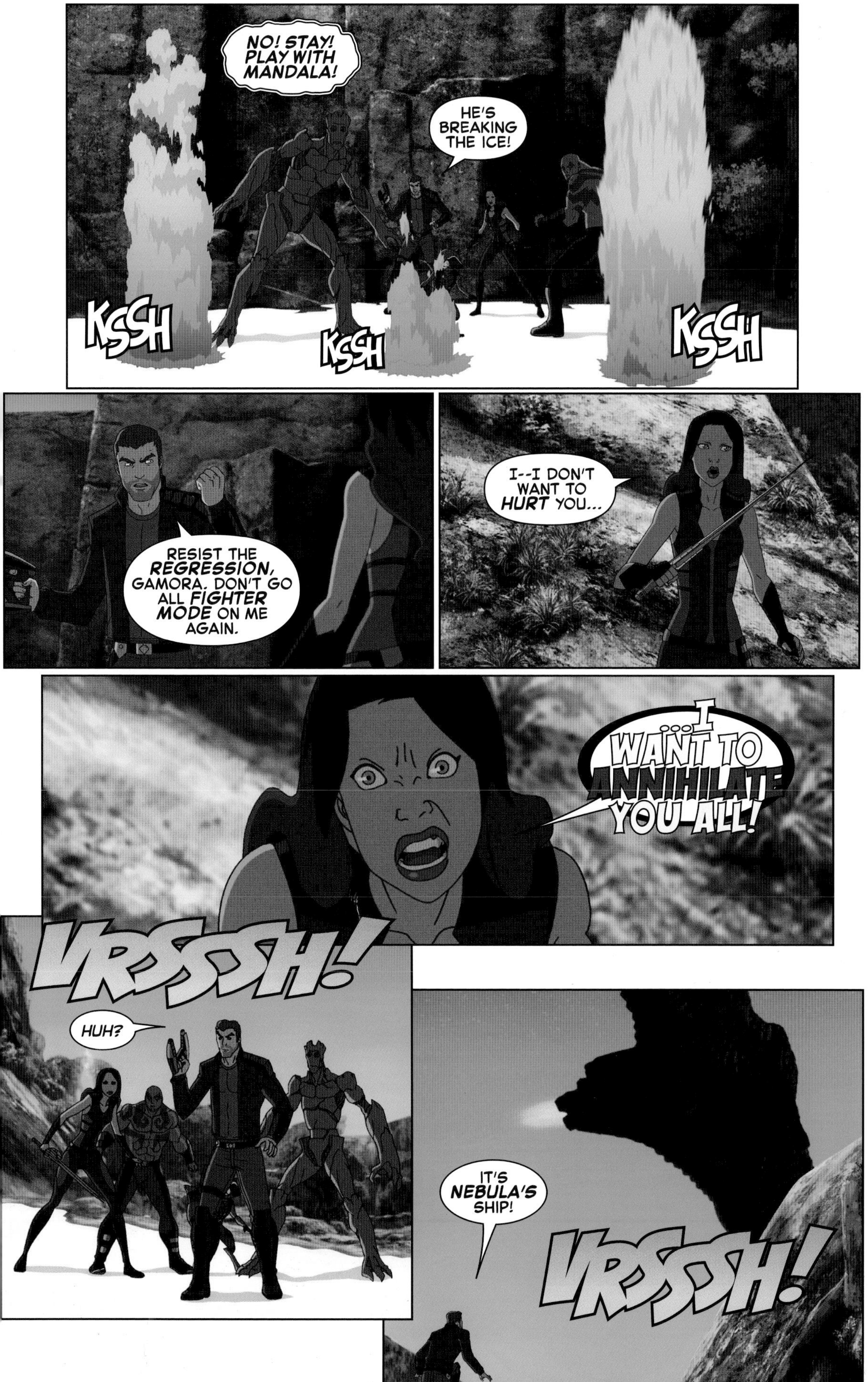
NO! STAY! PLAY WITH MANDALA!
HE'S BREAKING THE ICE!
KSSH
KSSH
KSSH
RESIST THE REGRESSION, GAMORA. DON'T GO ALL FIGHTER MODE ON ME AGAIN.
I--I DON'T WANT TO HURT YOU...
...I WANT TO ANNIHILATE YOU ALL!
VRSSSH!
HUH?
IT'S NEBULA'S SHIP!
VRSSSH!

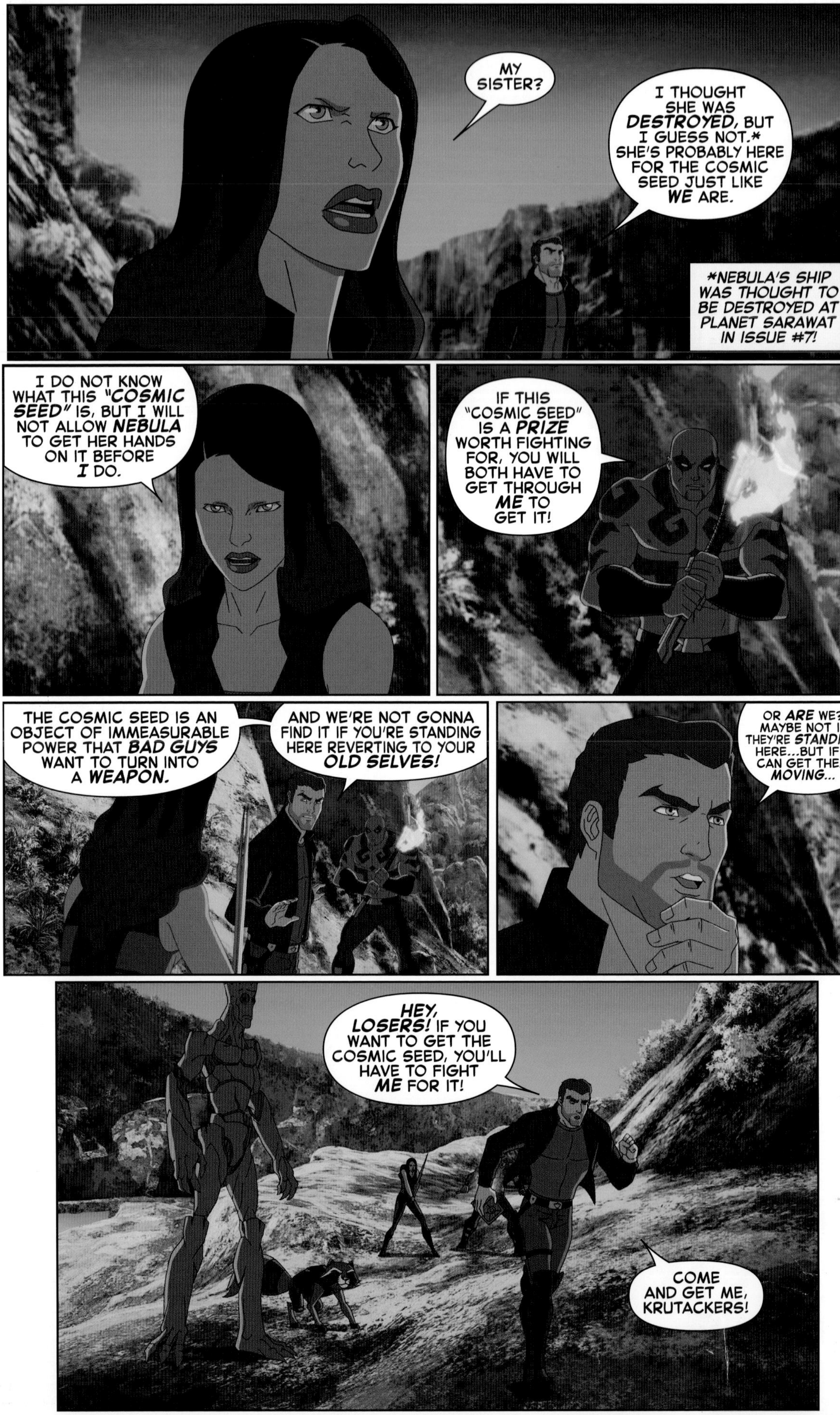
MY SISTER?
I THOUGHT SHE WAS *DESTROYED*, BUT I GUESS NOT.* SHE'S PROBABLY HERE FOR THE COSMIC SEED JUST LIKE *WE* ARE.
*NEBULA'S SHIP WAS THOUGHT TO BE DESTROYED AT PLANET SARAWAT IN ISSUE #7!
I DO NOT KNOW WHAT THIS *"COSMIC SEED"* IS, BUT I WILL NOT ALLOW *NEBULA* TO GET HER HANDS ON IT BEFORE *I* DO.
IF THIS "COSMIC SEED" IS A *PRIZE* WORTH FIGHTING FOR, YOU WILL BOTH HAVE TO GET THROUGH *ME* TO GET IT!
THE COSMIC SEED IS AN OBJECT OF IMMEASURABLE POWER THAT *BAD GUYS* WANT TO TURN INTO A *WEAPON.*
AND WE'RE NOT GONNA FIND IT IF YOU'RE STANDING HERE REVERTING TO YOUR *OLD SELVES!*
OR *ARE* WE? MAYBE NOT IF THEY'RE *STANDING* HERE...BUT IF I CAN GET THEM *MOVING*...
HEY, LOSERS! IF YOU WANT TO GET THE COSMIC SEED, YOU'LL HAVE TO FIGHT *ME* FOR IT!
COME AND GET ME, KRUTACKERS!

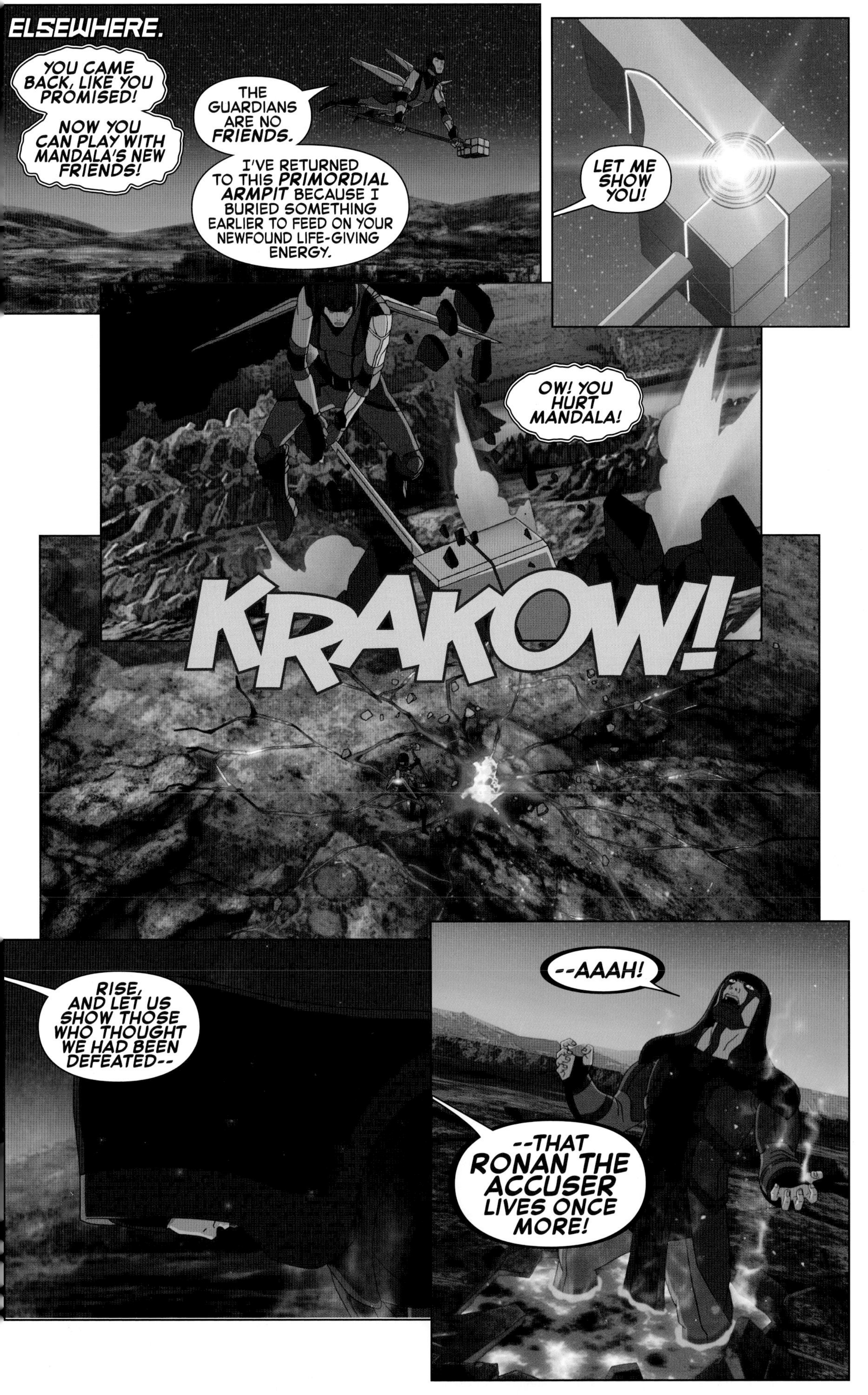
ELSEWHERE.
YOU CAME BACK, LIKE YOU PROMISED!
NOW YOU CAN PLAY WITH MANDALA'S NEW FRIENDS!
THE GUARDIANS ARE NO FRIENDS.
I'VE RETURNED TO THIS PRIMORDIAL ARMPIT BECAUSE I BURIED SOMETHING EARLIER TO FEED ON YOUR NEWFOUND LIFE-GIVING ENERGY.
LET ME SHOW YOU!
OW! YOU HURT MANDALA!
KRAKOW!
RISE, AND LET US SHOW THOSE WHO THOUGHT WE HAD BEEN DEFEATED--
--AAAH!
--THAT RONAN THE ACCUSER LIVES ONCE MORE!

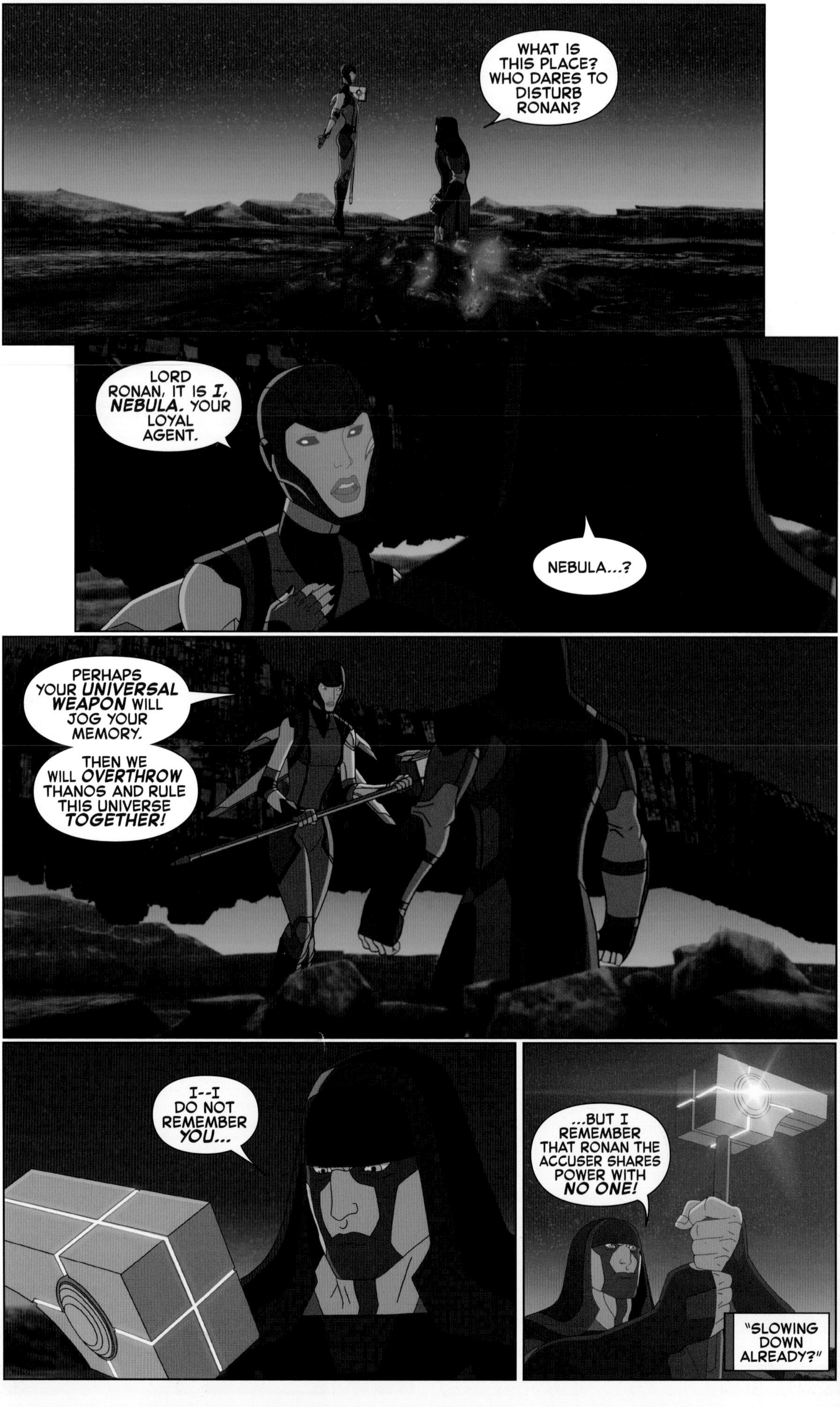
WHAT IS THIS PLACE? WHO DARES TO DISTURB RONAN?
LORD RONAN, IT IS *I*, ***NEBULA.*** YOUR LOYAL AGENT.
NEBULA...?
PERHAPS YOUR ***UNIVERSAL WEAPON*** WILL JOG YOUR MEMORY.
THEN WE WILL ***OVERTHROW*** THANOS AND RULE THIS UNIVERSE ***TOGETHER!***
I--I DO NOT REMEMBER ***YOU...***
...BUT I REMEMBER THAT RONAN THE ACCUSER SHARES POWER WITH ***NO ONE!***
"SLOWING DOWN ALREADY?"

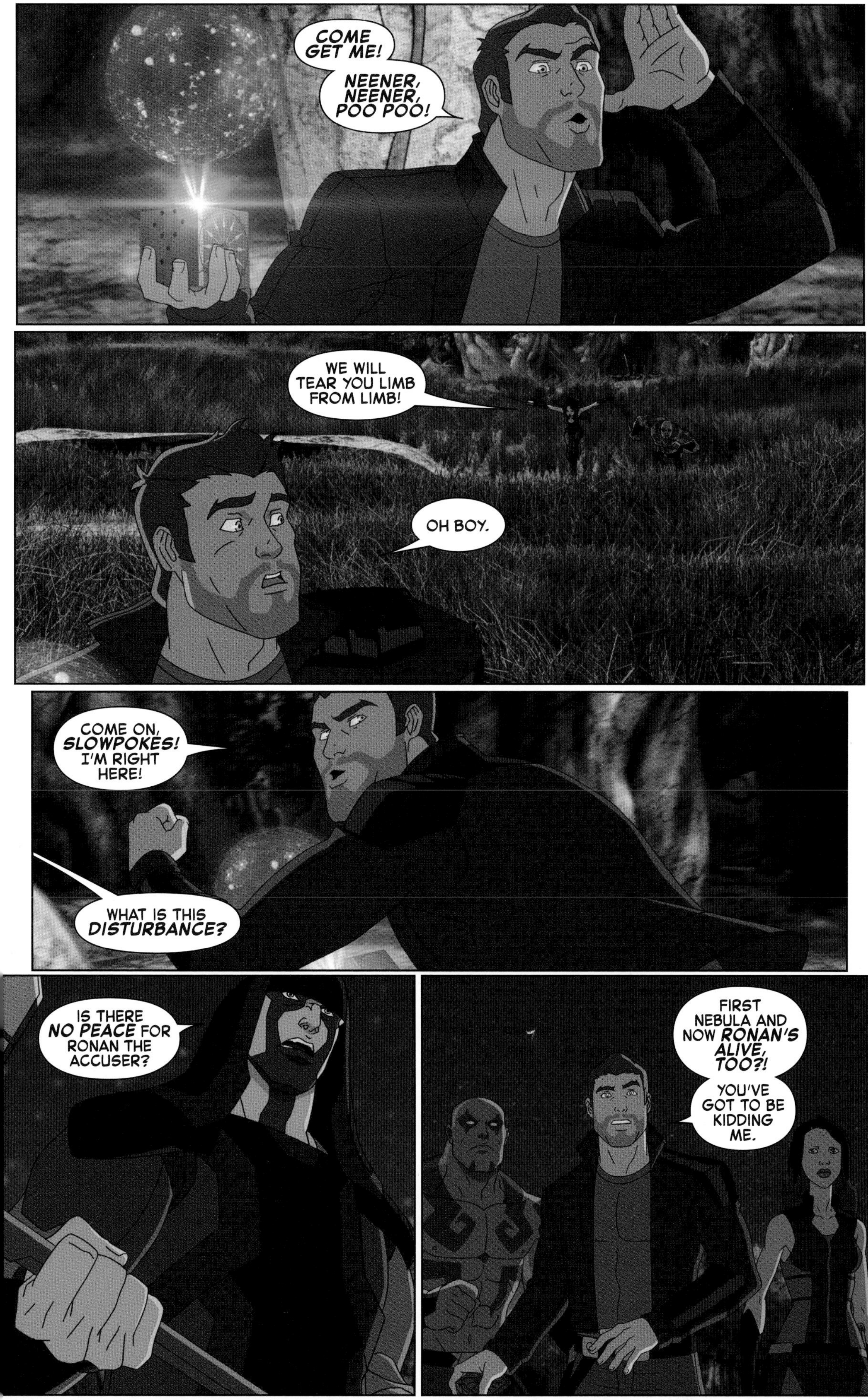
COME GET ME!
NEENER, NEENER, POO POO!
WE WILL TEAR YOU LIMB FROM LIMB!
OH BOY.
COME ON, SLOWPOKES! I'M RIGHT HERE!
WHAT IS THIS DISTURBANCE?
IS THERE NO PEACE FOR RONAN THE ACCUSER?
FIRST NEBULA AND NOW RONAN'S ALIVE, TOO?!
YOU'VE GOT TO BE KIDDING ME.

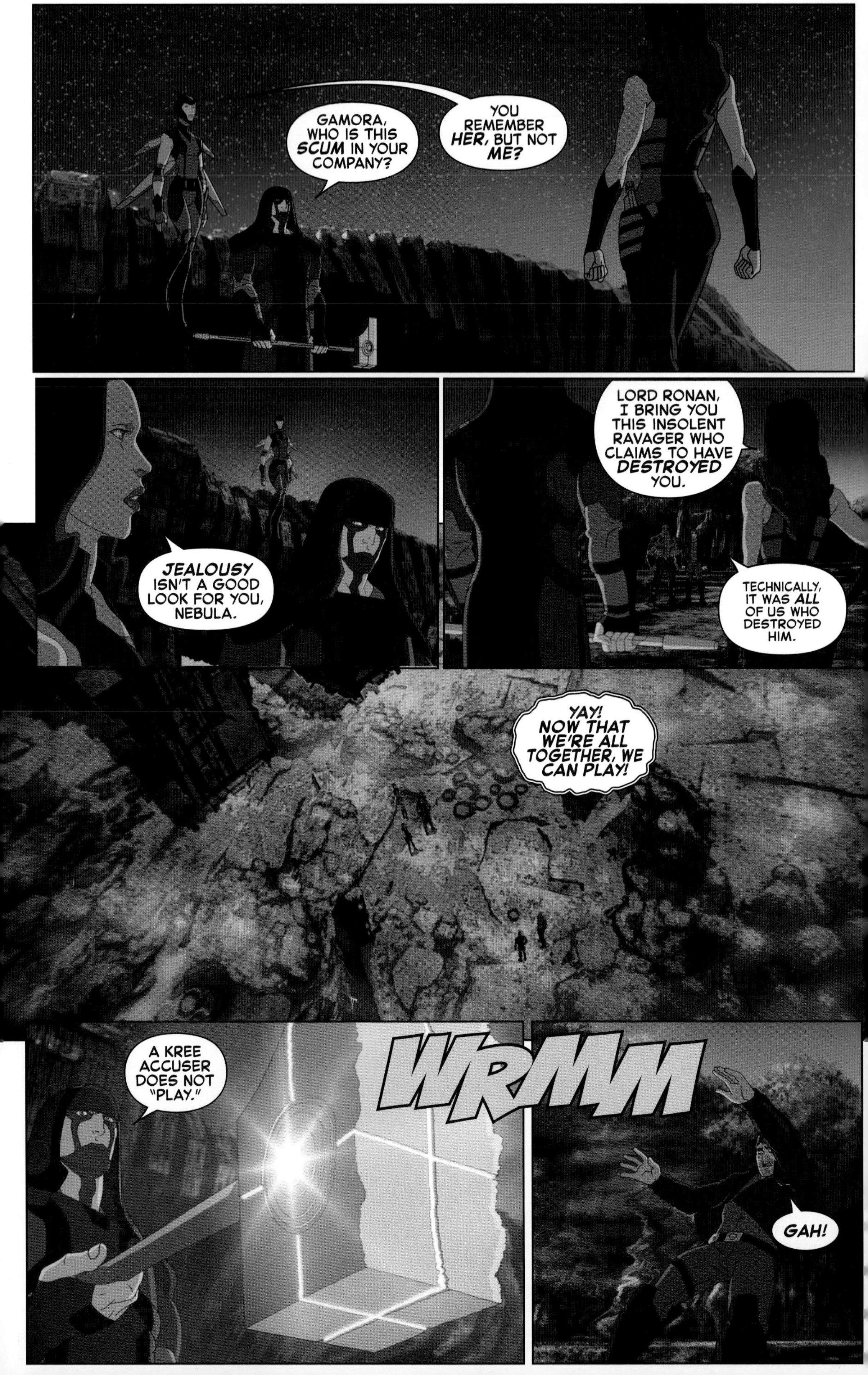
GAMORA, WHO IS THIS SCUM IN YOUR COMPANY?
YOU REMEMBER HER, BUT NOT ME?
JEALOUSY ISN'T A GOOD LOOK FOR YOU, NEBULA.
LORD RONAN, I BRING YOU THIS INSOLENT RAVAGER WHO CLAIMS TO HAVE DESTROYED YOU.
TECHNICALLY, IT WAS ALL OF US WHO DESTROYED HIM.
YAY! NOW THAT WE'RE ALL TOGETHER, WE CAN PLAY!
A KREE ACCUSER DOES NOT "PLAY."
WRMMM
GAH!

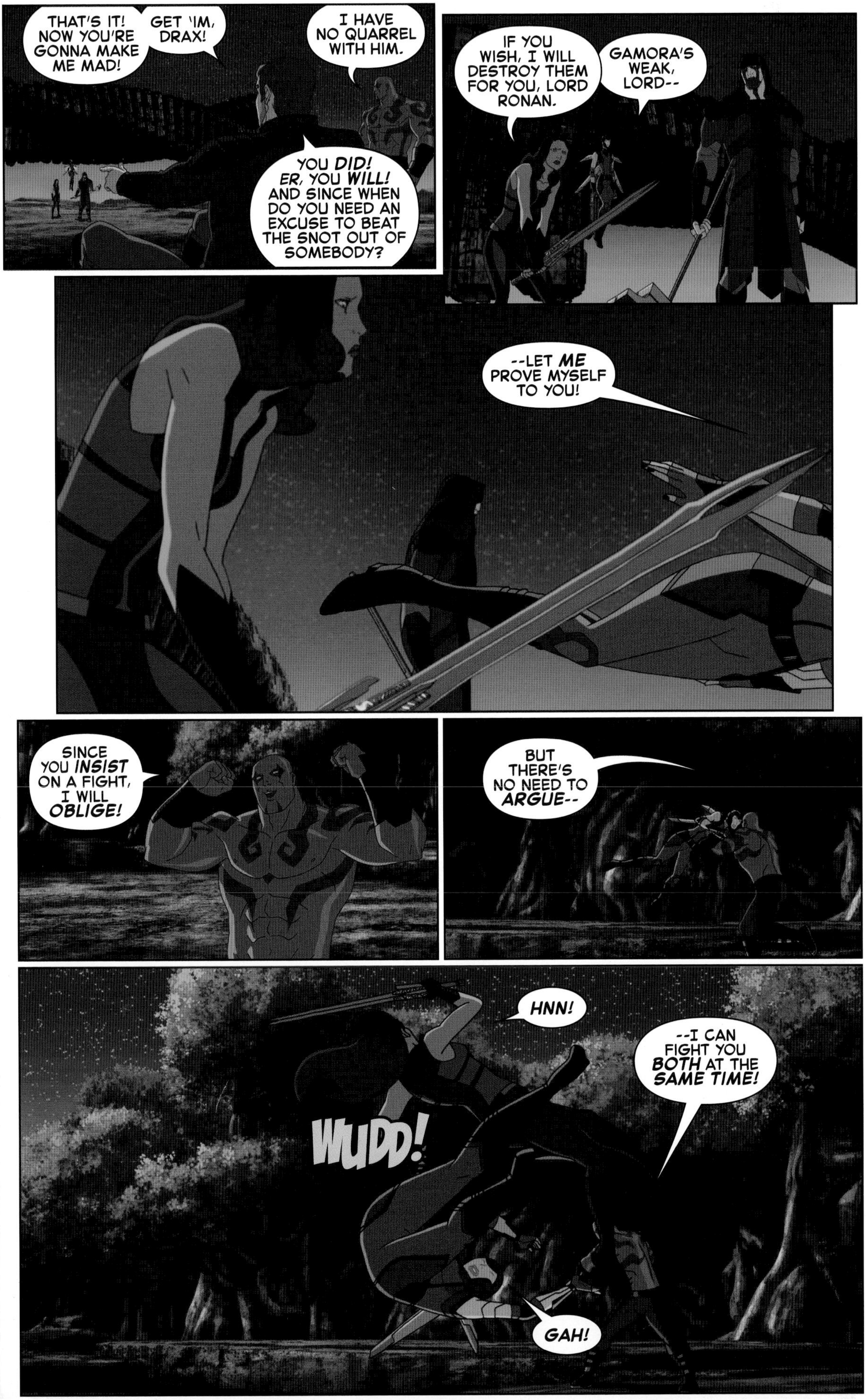

THAT'S IT! NOW YOU'RE GONNA MAKE ME MAD!
GET 'IM, DRAX!
I HAVE NO QUARREL WITH HIM.
YOU DID! ER, YOU WILL! AND SINCE WHEN DO YOU NEED AN EXCUSE TO BEAT THE SNOT OUT OF SOMEBODY?
IF YOU WISH, I WILL DESTROY THEM FOR YOU, LORD RONAN.
GAMORA'S WEAK, LORD--
--LET ME PROVE MYSELF TO YOU!
SINCE YOU INSIST ON A FIGHT, I WILL OBLIGE!
BUT THERE'S NO NEED TO ARGUE--
HNN!
--I CAN FIGHT YOU BOTH AT THE SAME TIME!
WUDD!
GAH!

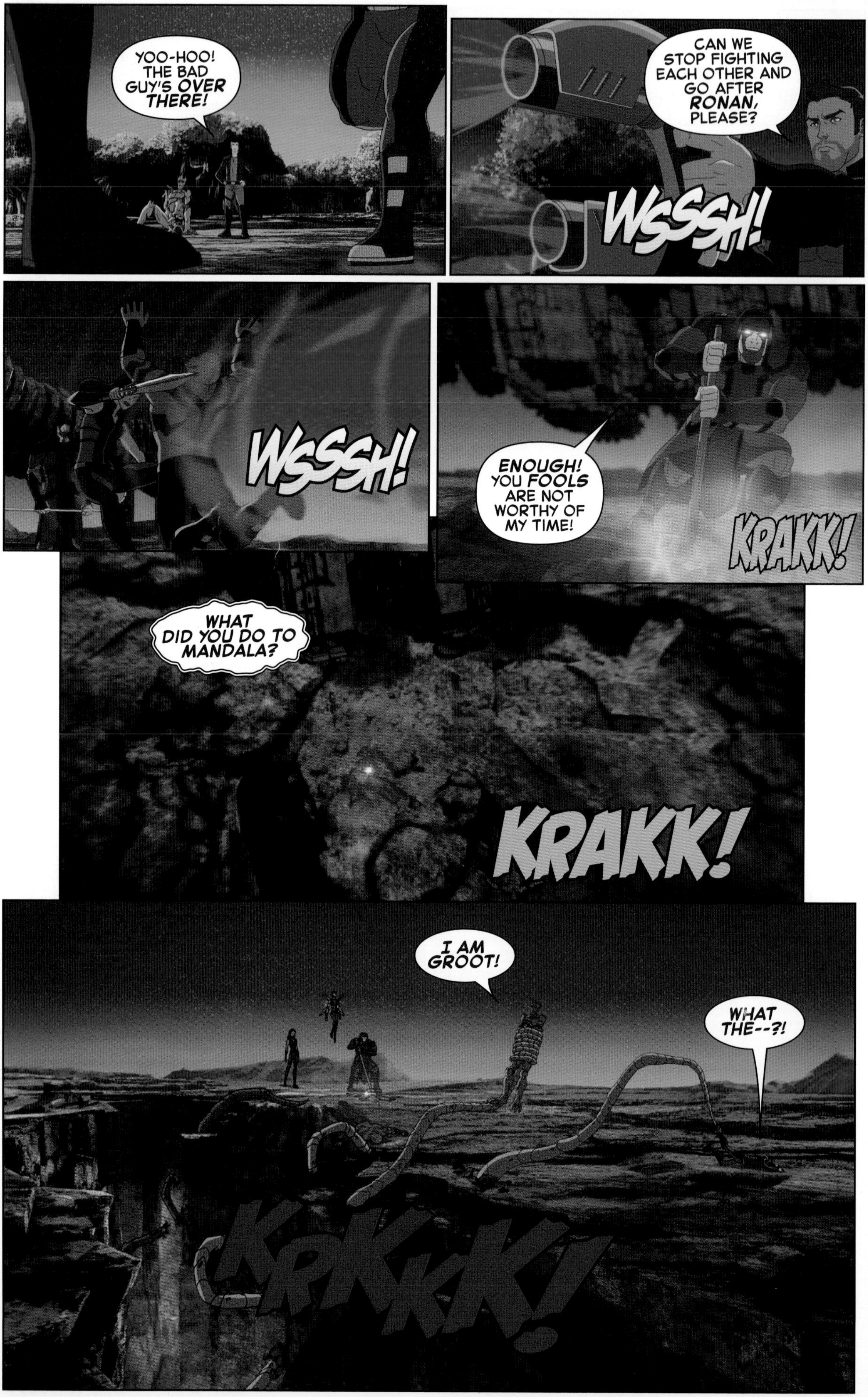
YOO-HOO! THE BAD GUY'S OVER THERE!
CAN WE STOP FIGHTING EACH OTHER AND GO AFTER RONAN, PLEASE?
WSSSH!
WSSSH!
ENOUGH! YOU FOOLS ARE NOT WORTHY OF MY TIME!
KRAKK!
WHAT DID YOU DO TO MANDALA?
KRAKK!
I AM GROOT!
WHAT THE--?!
KRKKK!

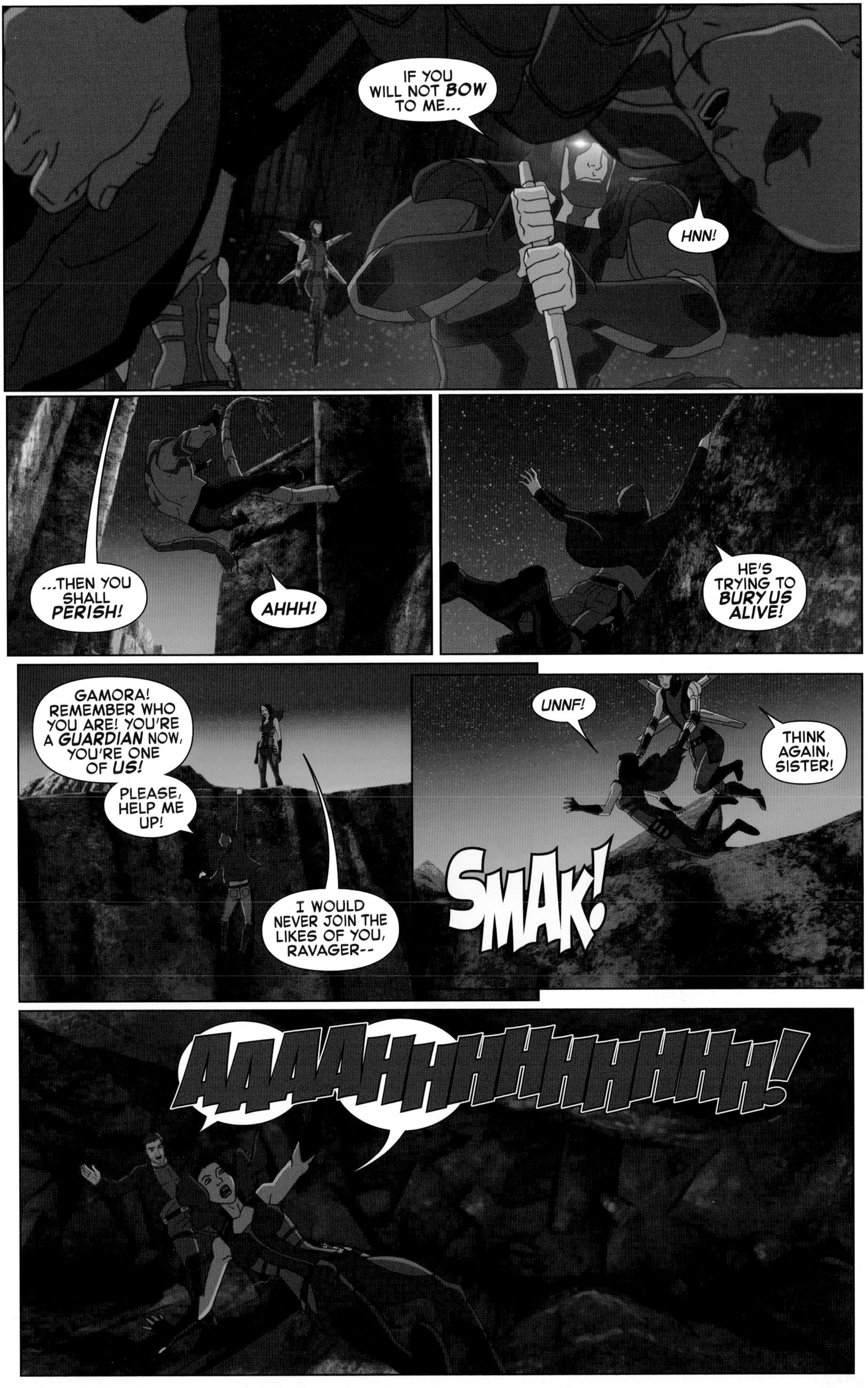
IF YOU WILL NOT BOW TO ME...
HNN!
...THEN YOU SHALL PERISH!
AHHH!
HE'S TRYING TO BURY US ALIVE!
GAMORA! REMEMBER WHO YOU ARE! YOU'RE A GUARDIAN NOW, YOU'RE ONE OF US!
PLEASE, HELP ME UP!
I WOULD NEVER JOIN THE LIKES OF YOU, RAVAGER--
UNNF!
THINK AGAIN, SISTER!
SMAK!
AAAAHHHHHHHHHH!

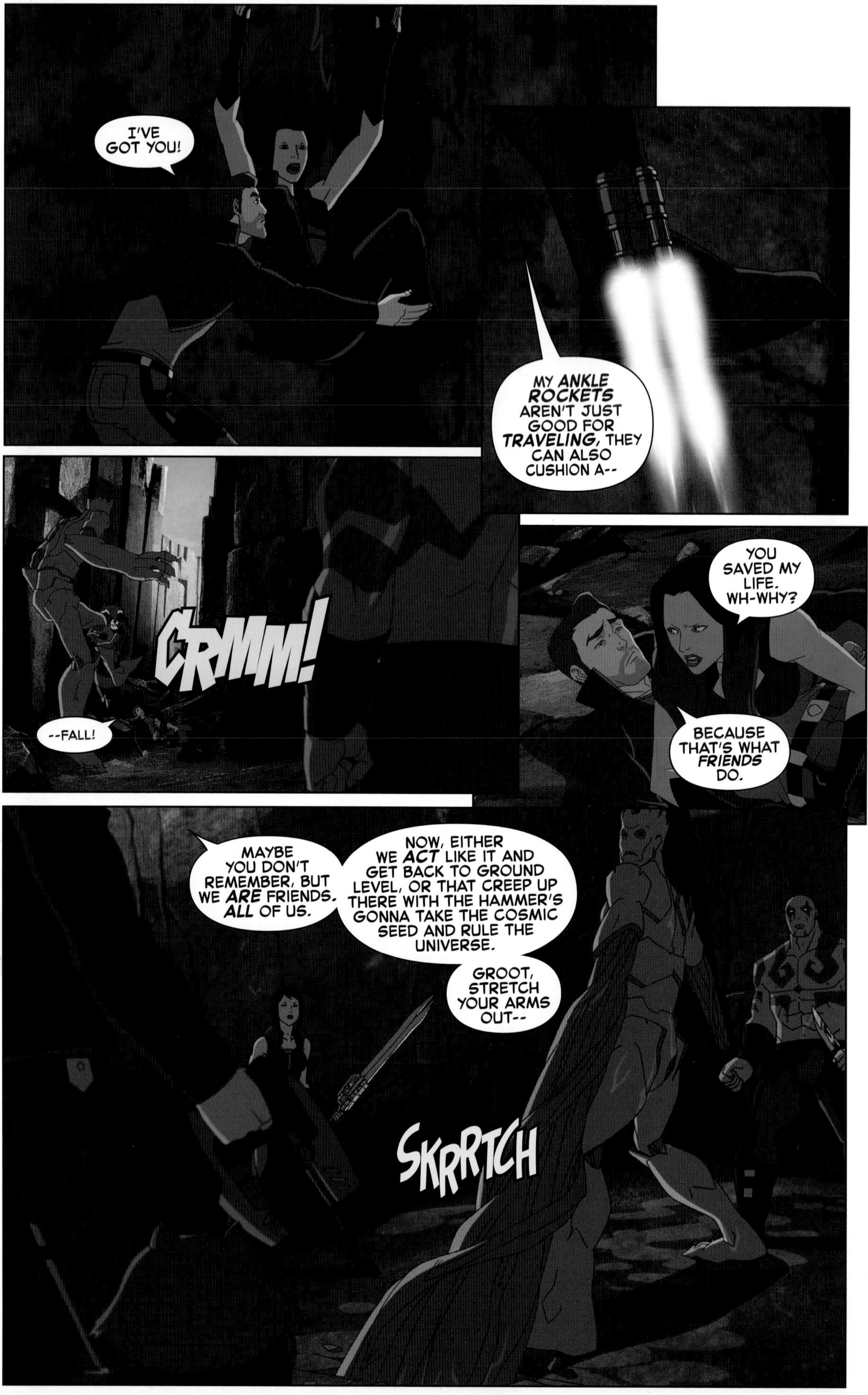
I'VE GOT YOU!
MY ANKLE ROCKETS AREN'T JUST GOOD FOR TRAVELING, THEY CAN ALSO CUSHION A--
CRMM!
--FALL!
YOU SAVED MY LIFE. WH-WHY?
BECAUSE THAT'S WHAT FRIENDS DO.
MAYBE YOU DON'T REMEMBER, BUT WE ARE FRIENDS. ALL OF US.
NOW, EITHER WE ACT LIKE IT AND GET BACK TO GROUND LEVEL, OR THAT CREEP UP THERE WITH THE HAMMER'S GONNA TAKE THE COSMIC SEED AND RULE THE UNIVERSE.
GROOT, STRETCH YOUR ARMS OUT--
SKRRTCH

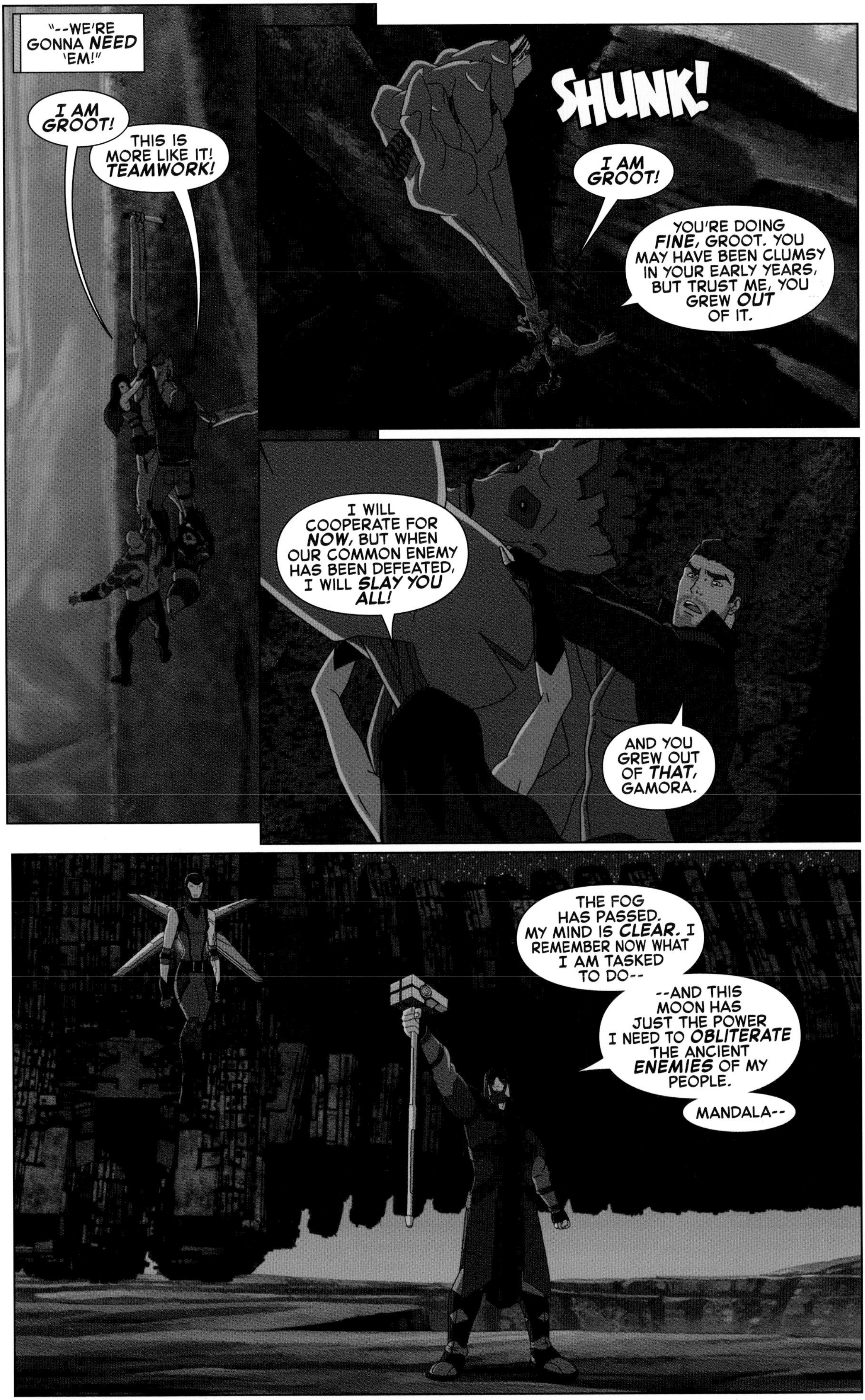
"--WE'RE GONNA NEED 'EM!"
I AM GROOT!
THIS IS MORE LIKE IT! TEAMWORK!
SHUNK!
I AM GROOT!
YOU'RE DOING FINE, GROOT. YOU MAY HAVE BEEN CLUMSY IN YOUR EARLY YEARS, BUT TRUST ME, YOU GREW OUT OF IT.
I WILL COOPERATE FOR NOW, BUT WHEN OUR COMMON ENEMY HAS BEEN DEFEATED, I WILL SLAY YOU ALL!
AND YOU GREW OUT OF THAT, GAMORA.
THE FOG HAS PASSED. MY MIND IS CLEAR. I REMEMBER NOW WHAT I AM TASKED TO DO--
--AND THIS MOON HAS JUST THE POWER I NEED TO OBLITERATE THE ANCIENT ENEMIES OF MY PEOPLE.
MANDALA--

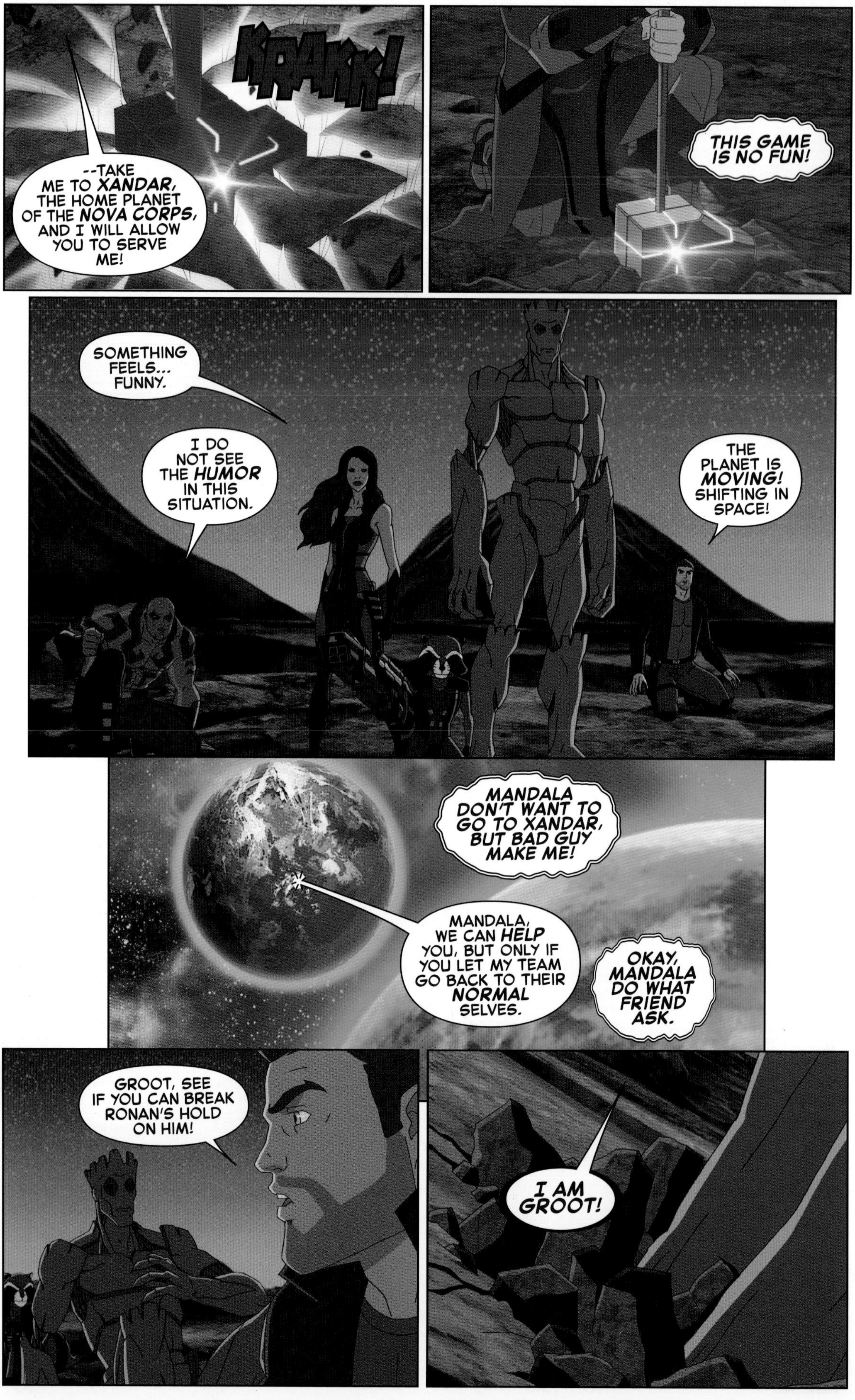
KRAKK!
--TAKE ME TO XANDAR, THE HOME PLANET OF THE NOVA CORPS, AND I WILL ALLOW YOU TO SERVE ME!
THIS GAME IS NO FUN!
SOMETHING FEELS... FUNNY.
I DO NOT SEE THE HUMOR IN THIS SITUATION.
THE PLANET IS MOVING! SHIFTING IN SPACE!
MANDALA DON'T WANT TO GO TO XANDAR, BUT BAD GUY MAKE ME!
MANDALA, WE CAN HELP YOU, BUT ONLY IF YOU LET MY TEAM GO BACK TO THEIR NORMAL SELVES.
OKAY, MANDALA DO WHAT FRIEND ASK.
GROOT, SEE IF YOU CAN BREAK RONAN'S HOLD ON HIM!
I AM GROOT!

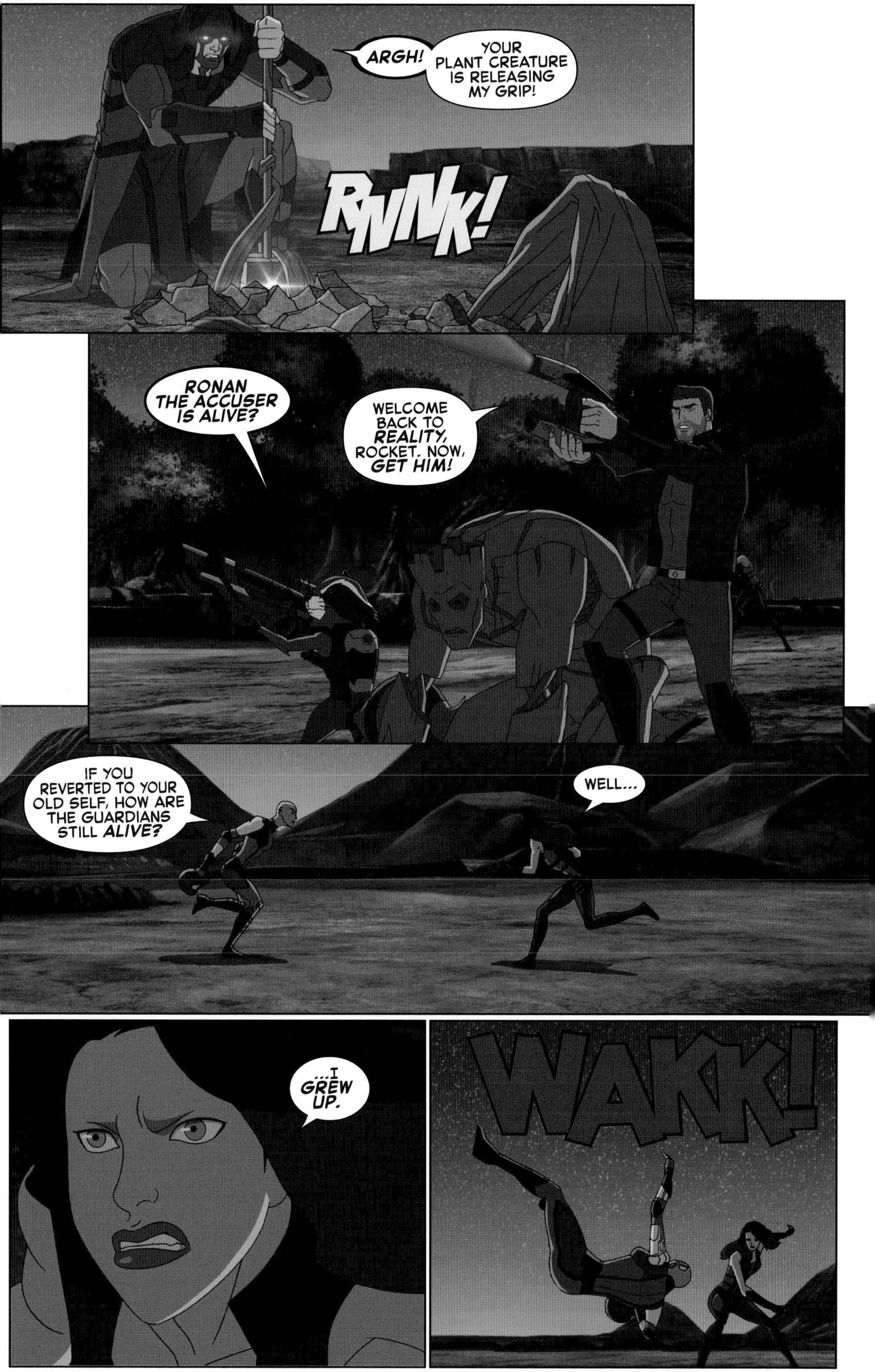
ARGH!
YOUR PLANT CREATURE IS RELEASING MY GRIP!
RANK!
RONAN THE ACCUSER IS ALIVE?
WELCOME BACK TO REALITY, ROCKET. NOW, GET HIM!
IF YOU REVERTED TO YOUR OLD SELF, HOW ARE THE GUARDIANS STILL ALIVE?
WELL...
...I GREW UP.
WAKK!

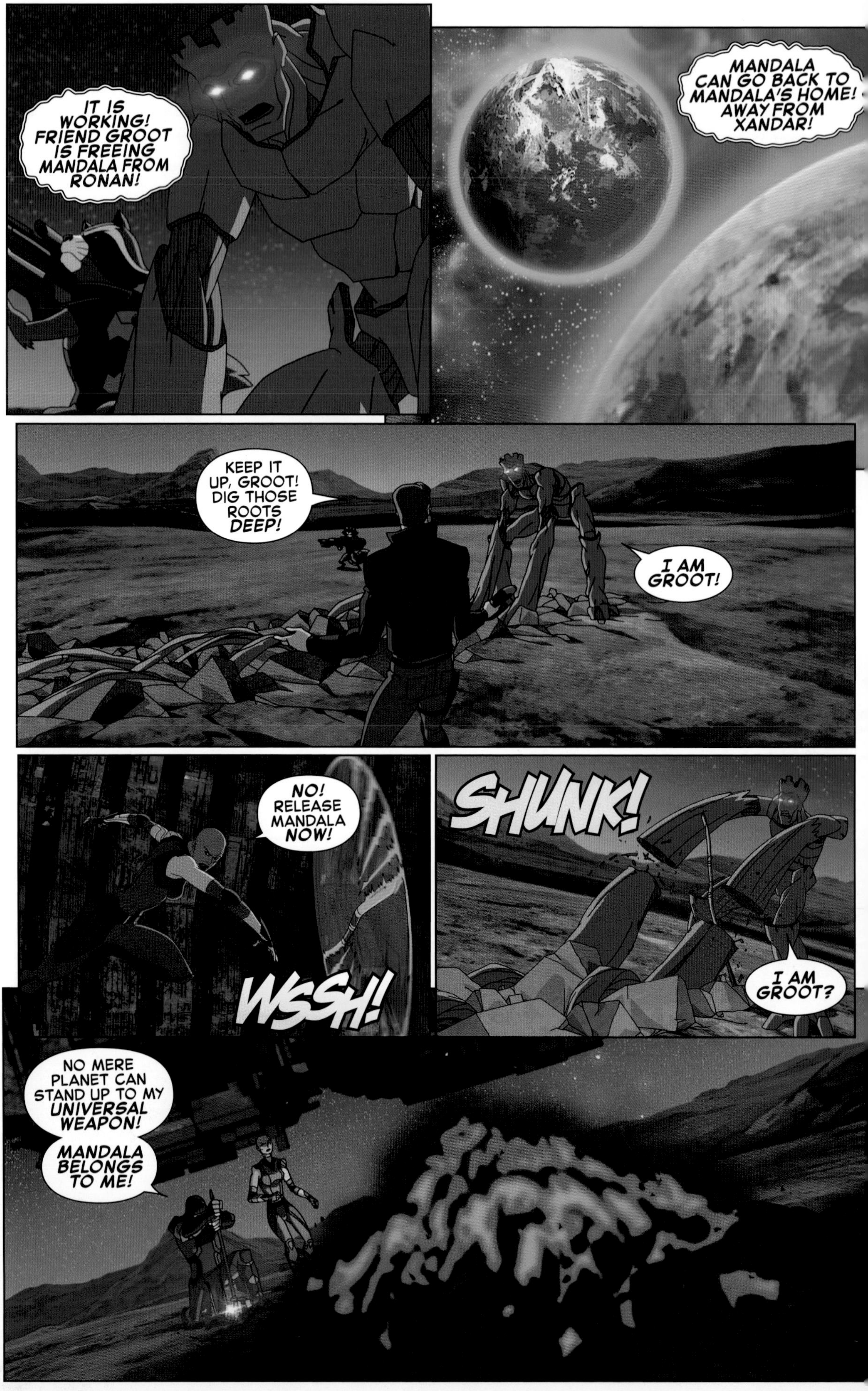
IT IS WORKING! FRIEND GROOT IS FREEING MANDALA FROM RONAN!
MANDALA CAN GO BACK TO MANDALA'S HOME! AWAY FROM XANDAR!
KEEP IT UP, GROOT! DIG THOSE ROOTS DEEP!
I AM GROOT!
NO! RELEASE MANDALA NOW!
WSSH!
SHUNK!
I AM GROOT?
NO MERE PLANET CAN STAND UP TO MY UNIVERSAL WEAPON!
MANDALA BELONGS TO ME!

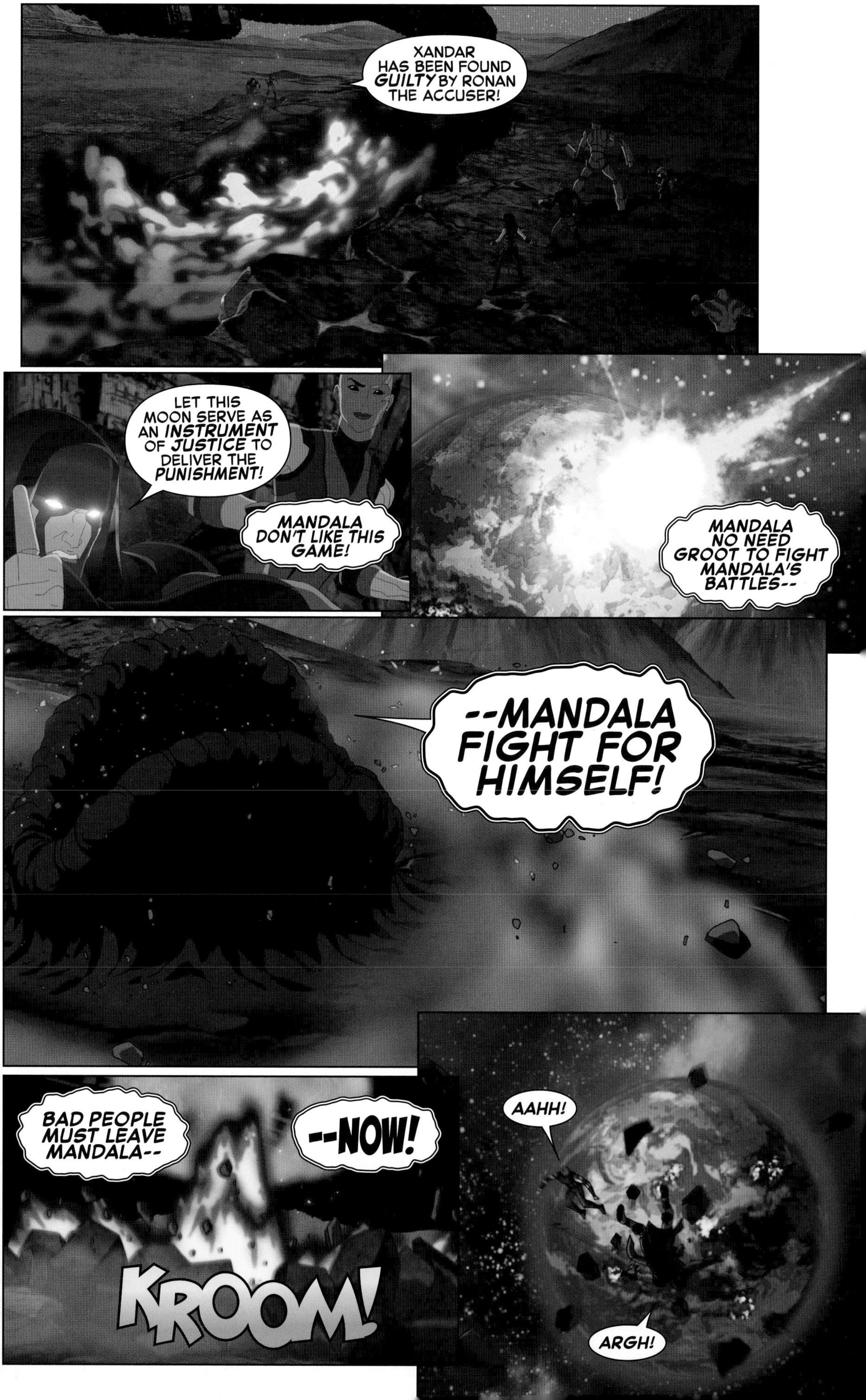
XANDAR HAS BEEN FOUND GUILTY BY RONAN THE ACCUSER!
LET THIS MOON SERVE AS AN INSTRUMENT OF JUSTICE TO DELIVER THE PUNISHMENT!
MANDALA DON'T LIKE THIS GAME!
MANDALA NO NEED GROOT TO FIGHT MANDALA'S BATTLES--
--MANDALA FIGHT FOR HIMSELF!
BAD PEOPLE MUST LEAVE MANDALA--
--NOW!
KROOM!
AAHH!
ARGH!

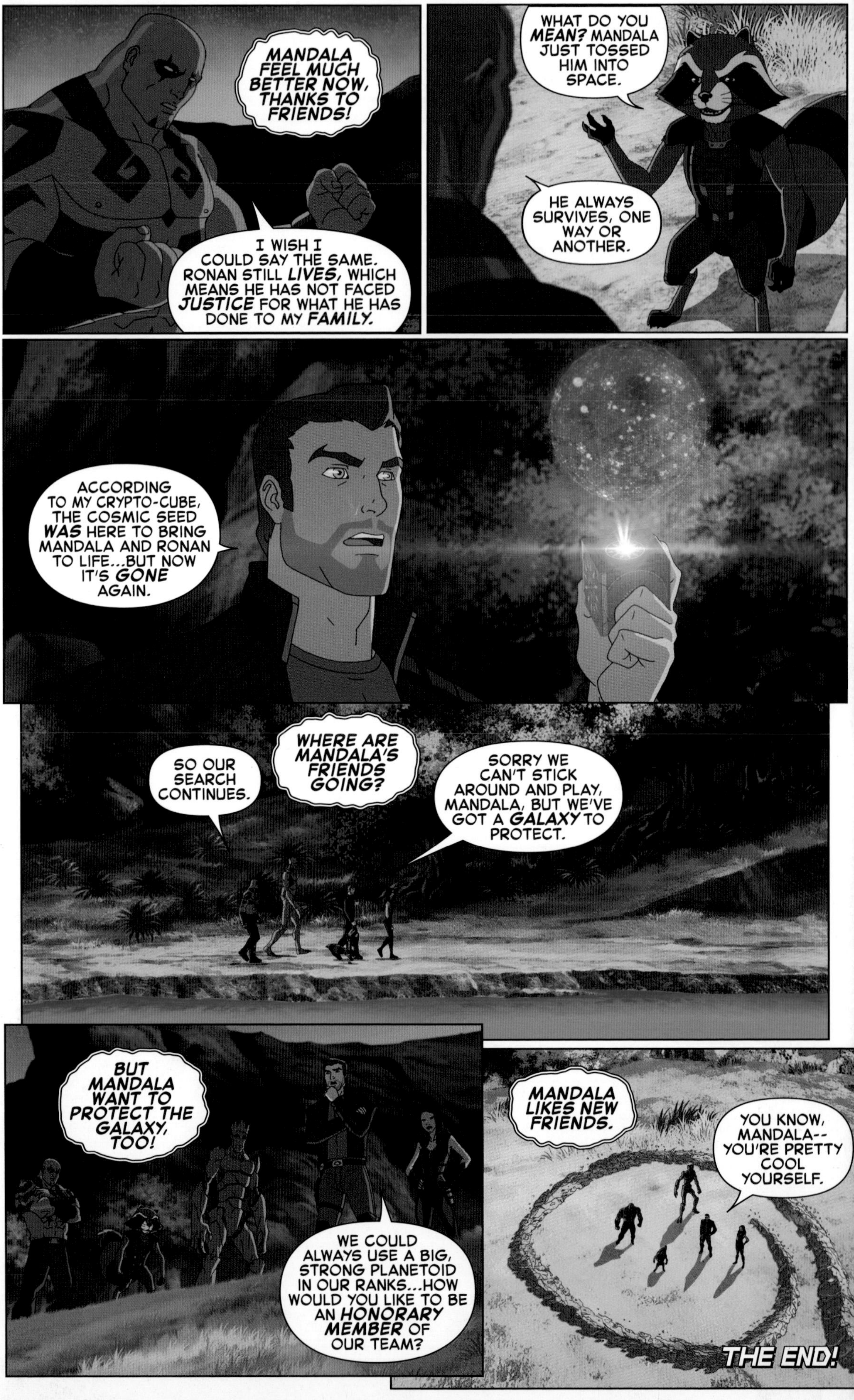
MANDALA FEEL MUCH BETTER NOW, THANKS TO FRIENDS!
I WISH I COULD SAY THE SAME. RONAN STILL LIVES, WHICH MEANS HE HAS NOT FACED JUSTICE FOR WHAT HE HAS DONE TO MY FAMILY.
WHAT DO YOU MEAN? MANDALA JUST TOSSED HIM INTO SPACE.
HE ALWAYS SURVIVES, ONE WAY OR ANOTHER.
ACCORDING TO MY CRYPTO-CUBE, THE COSMIC SEED WAS HERE TO BRING MANDALA AND RONAN TO LIFE...BUT NOW IT'S GONE AGAIN.
SO OUR SEARCH CONTINUES.
WHERE ARE MANDALA'S FRIENDS GOING?
SORRY WE CAN'T STICK AROUND AND PLAY, MANDALA, BUT WE'VE GOT A GALAXY TO PROTECT.
BUT MANDALA WANT TO PROTECT THE GALAXY, TOO!
WE COULD ALWAYS USE A BIG, STRONG PLANETOID IN OUR RANKS...HOW WOULD YOU LIKE TO BE AN HONORARY MEMBER OF OUR TEAM?
MANDALA LIKES NEW FRIENDS.
YOU KNOW, MANDALA-- YOU'RE PRETTY COOL YOURSELF.
THE END!

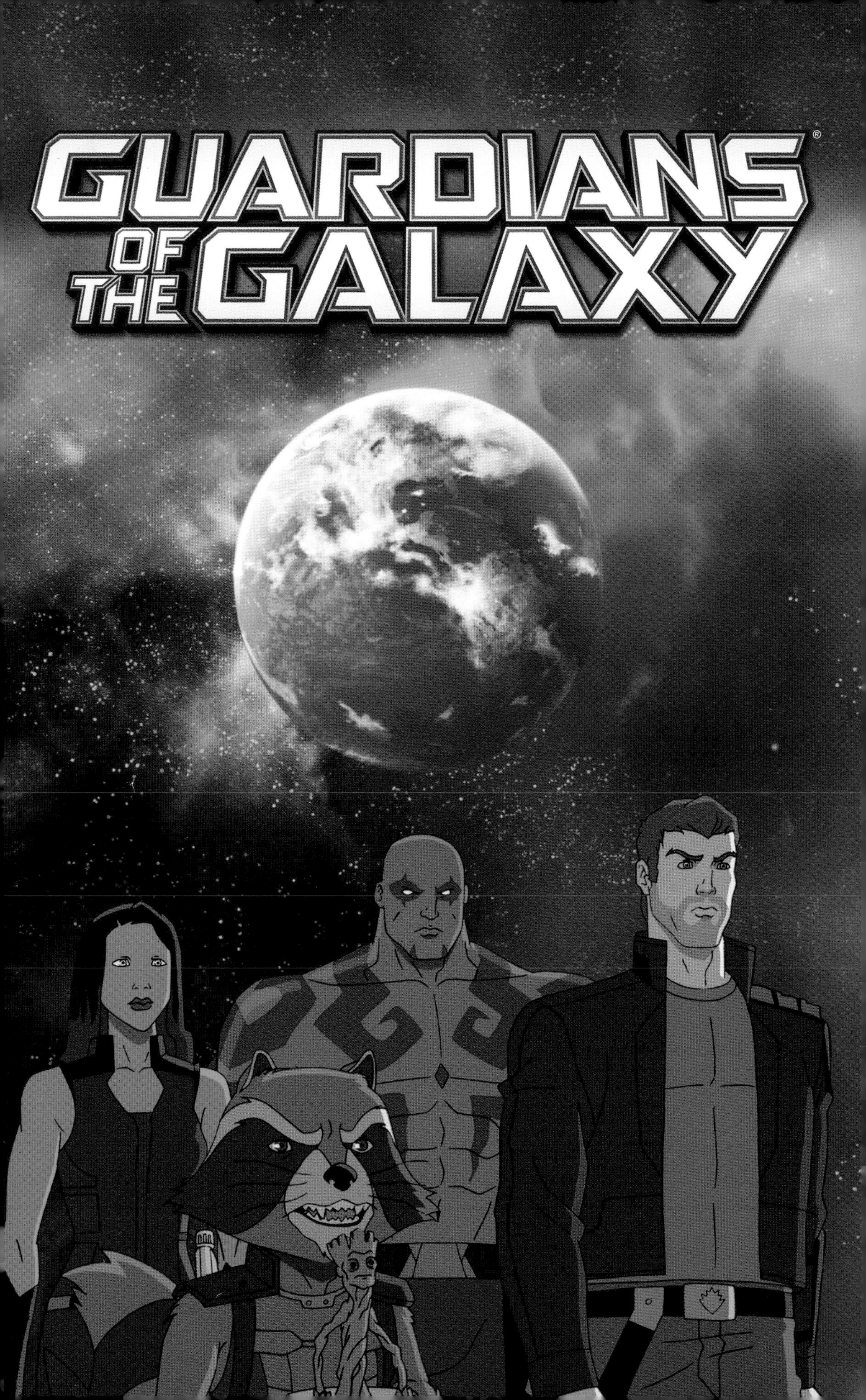
GUARDIANS OF THE GALAXY

GUARDIANS OF THE GALAXY

COLLECT THEM ALL!

Set of 6 Hardcover Books ISBN: 978-1-5321-4357-1

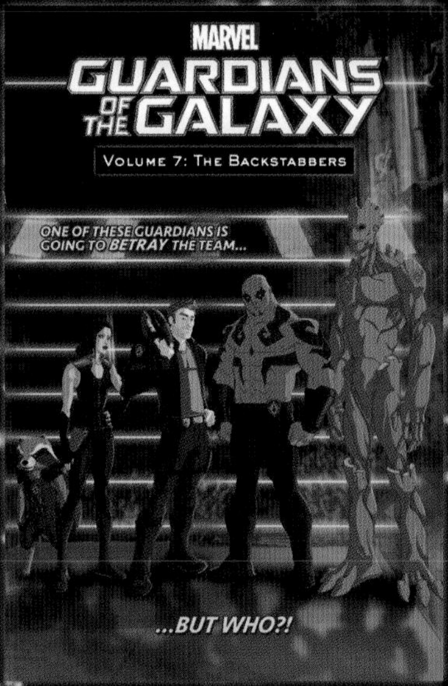
MARVEL
GUARDIANS OF THE GALAXY
VOLUME 7: THE BACKSTABBERS
ONE OF THESE GUARDIANS IS GOING TO BETRAY THE TEAM...
...BUT WHO?!

Hardcover Book ISBN
978-1-5321-4358-8

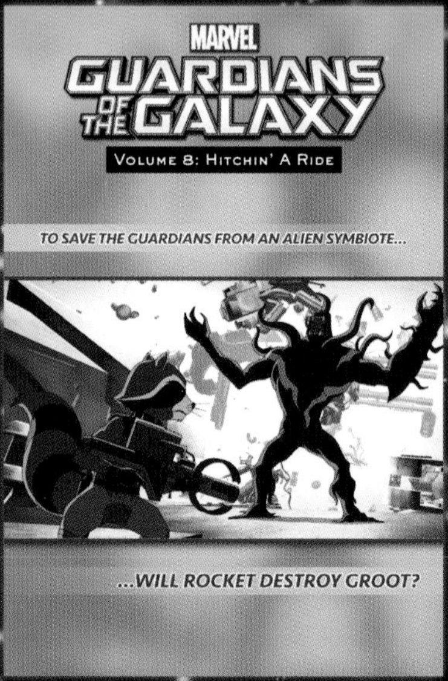
MARVEL
GUARDIANS OF THE GALAXY
VOLUME 8: HITCHIN' A RIDE
TO SAVE THE GUARDIANS FROM AN ALIEN SYMBIOTE...
...WILL ROCKET DESTROY GROOT?

Hardcover Book ISBN
978-1-5321-4359-5

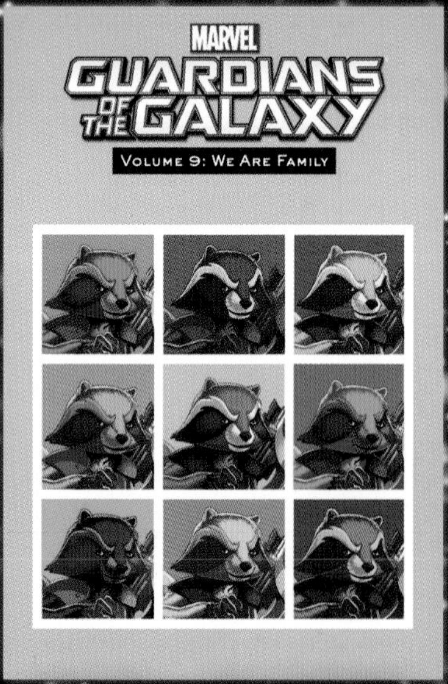
MARVEL
GUARDIANS OF THE GALAXY
VOLUME 9: WE ARE FAMILY

Hardcover Book ISBN
978-1-5321-4360-1

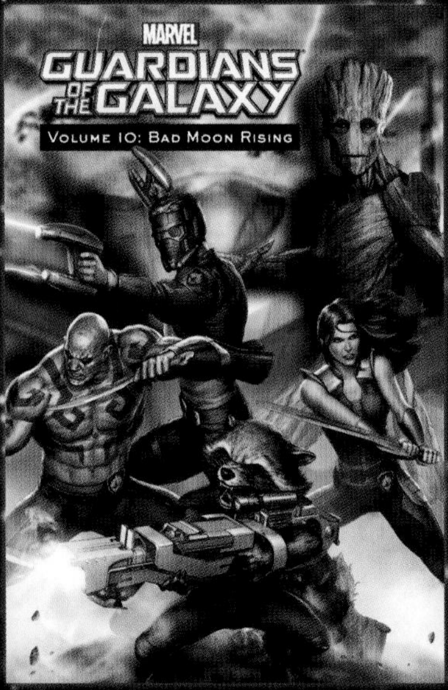
MARVEL
GUARDIANS OF THE GALAXY
VOLUME 10: BAD MOON RISING

Hardcover Book ISBN
978-1-5321-4361-8

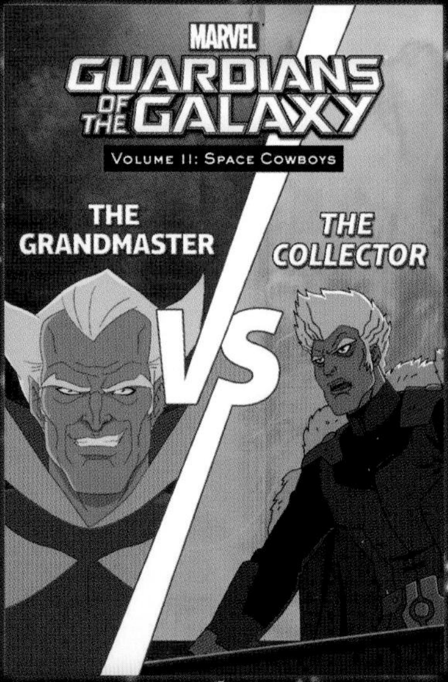
MARVEL
GUARDIANS OF THE GALAXY
VOLUME 11: SPACE COWBOYS
THE GRANDMASTER
VS
THE COLLECTOR

Hardcover Book ISBN
978-1-5321-4362-5

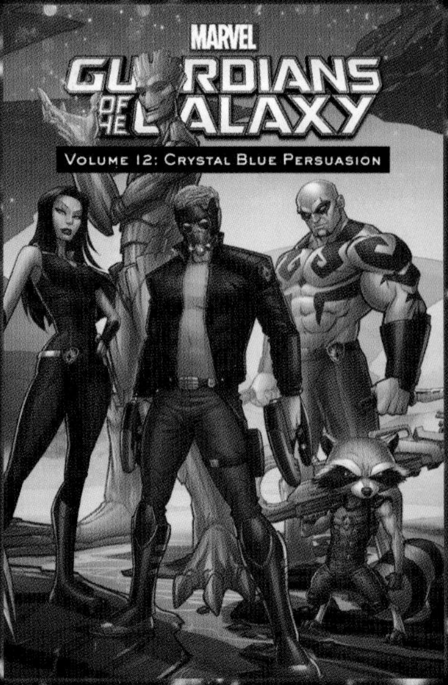
MARVEL
VOLUME 12: CRYSTAL BLUE PERSUASION

Hardcover Book ISBN
978-1-5321-4363-2